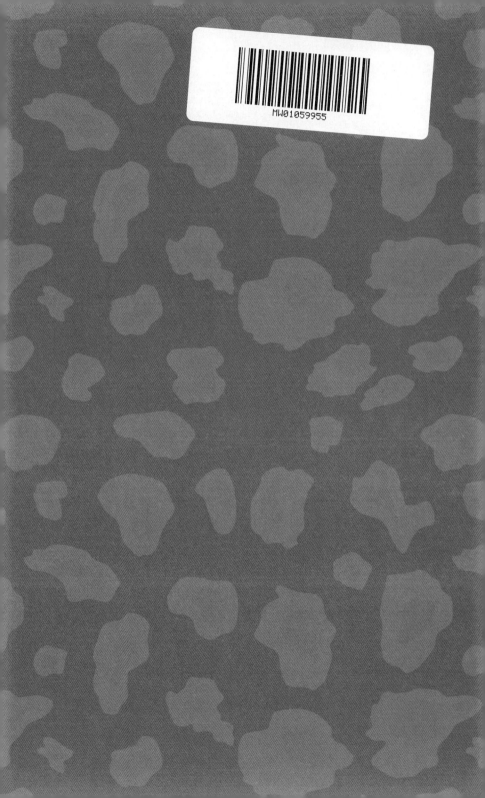

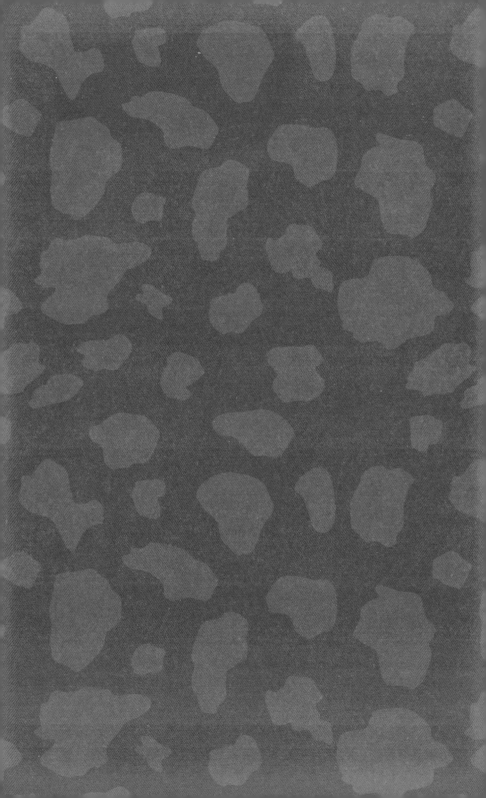

This book belongs to . . .

Saurie   Tohnson

Stock photos ©: 11 chair: IGORdeyka/Shutterstock; 11 tree: www.freevector.com;
49 background, 82-83 border, 88 envelope: Created by Freepik.

© 2019 Ty Inc. Used with permission of Ty Inc. TY and the TY Heart Logo are registered trademarks
of Ty Inc. The trademark BEANIE BOOS™ is also owned by Ty Inc.

ISBN 978-1-338-28586-4

10 9 8 7 6 5 4 3 2 1   19 20 21 22 23

Printed in China   68

First edition, May 2019

Book design by Becky James

FRIENDSHIP FUR-EVER

Journal

by Marilyn Easton

SCHOLASTIC INC.

All About You

My name is . . .

My favorite animal is . . .

I love eating . . .

My favorite song is . . .

My favorite color is . . .

I love saying . . .

sweet

love it ♥

My favorite book is . . .

My favorite actress is . . .

My favorite actor is . . .

I love to play . . .

My favorite ice-cream flavor is . . .

My favorite candy is . . .

I love going to . . .

I love visiting . . .

My favorite musician is . . .

My favorite Beanie Boo is . . .

BFFs!

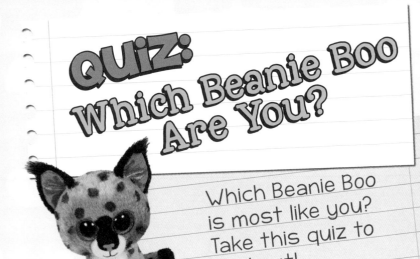

QUIZ: Which Beanie Boo Are You?

Which Beanie Boo is most like you? Take this quiz to find out!

1 If you could live anywhere, it would be:

a. On an island
b. In the Arctic
c. Under the sea
d. In a sunny spot
e. In a big city

2 Your friends would describe you as:

a. Easygoing
b. Sweet and shy
c. Cheerful and kind
d. Wild and fun
e. Smart and helpful

3 You can do anything you want on Saturday afternoon. You decide to:
a. Go to a party
b. Play in the snow
c. Make a flower bouquet for a friend
d. Listen to your favorite band
e. Do your homework

 4 Your clothes are mostly:
a. Bold and bright
b. Classic neutrals
c. Florals and pinks
d. Stripes and polka dots
e. Plaid and preppy

 5 You love to:
a. Play games with your friends
b. Snuggle up in your bed
c. Give presents to your friends and family
d. Listen to loud music
e. Ace every test

Turn the page to find out which Beanie Boo you are most like!

QUIZ RESULTS

If you got mostly As...
You're easygoing and are always looking forward to hanging out with your friends, just like **Wynnie**. You're the first one to throw a party or challenge friends to a game.

If you got mostly Bs...
You're just like **Buckwheat**! Although you may be a little shy, your friends can always count on you to be there for them.

If you got mostly Cs . . .

You are just like **Rosie!** You're always down for a trip to the beach, and your friends love your cheerful attitude. If your pals need cheering up, they know you're the one to call.

If you got mostly Ds...

You have a rebellious side and a love for music, just like **Izzy**! You love sharing your latest playlist with friends and adore trying out new things.

If you got mostly Es...

You're a supersmart student with a passion for learning, just like **Tala**! You love hanging out with friends in study groups. After school, you can usually be found doing your homework.

Life on a Desert Island

Kiwi loves the island life. If you were stranded on a desert island, what are the five items you would bring with you?

1. BLahket
2. Food
3. water
4. Some tolke
5. Bote

I am 9

My own Beanie Boo

If you could create your very own Beanie Boo, what would he or she look like? Fill in your Boo's name, poem, and birthday here. Then draw your Boo!

Name: _____

Birthday: _____

Personal Poem: _____

_____

_____

_____

mine

Draw your
very own
Beanie Boo
here!

13

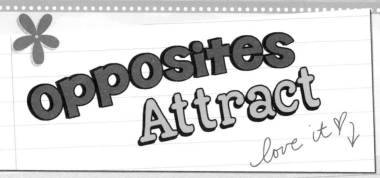

opposites Attract

love it ♡↓

Now take the Beanie Boo you just created and draw his or her exact opposite!

Name: _____

Birthday: _____

Personal Poem: _____

_____

_____

_____

BFFs!

Draw your
Beanie Boo's
opposite
here.

15

Elfie's favorite snack is peanuts! What are your top ten must-have snacks?

1. Candy
2. Chessets
3. Star bucks
4.
5.
6.
7.
8.
9.
10.

My Beanie Boo Superhero!

Swoops loves watching superhero movies. He even invented his own superhero, Super Bat!

Super Bat!

If you were a superhero, what would your name be? What superpowers would you have?

Superhero Name:

Superpowers:

Your Super Backstory:

Wow!

Shimmering Sky ♥ ✳

Ever wish you could visit Beanie Boo Land? There are so many magical places to explore. The Shimmering Sky is full of white, fluffy clouds; slides made out of rainbows; and a star-filled sky.

Draw this breezy location and some of the Beanie Boos who live there!

These Beanie Boos live in the Shimmering Sky:

Rosey   Darla   Halo

My Favorite Sport

love it ♡

Gilbert's favorite sport is volleyball. What's your favorite sport? Create a team for it!

Team Name:

Sport:

Team Members:

Team Mascot:

Design your team's uniform here!

Breaking Records

Who's climbed the tallest tree in Beanie Boo Land? Lizzie has! This tree-climbing leopard is proud of her record. Jot down your own achievements!

Number of Sports Played:

. . . .

Number of Books Read:

. . . .

Number of Teeth Lost:

. . . .

Number of Birthdays Celebrated:

. . . .

Number of Cupcakes Baked:

. . . .

Number of Flowers Planted:

. . . .

Number of Shoes Lost:

. . . .

Number of Pets Owned:

. . . .

Babs loves window-shopping. What are your top ten favorite shops? List them here!

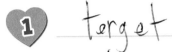

1. target
2. clars
3. cosko
4. Amizon
5.
6. Dickss
7.
8.
9.
10.

Game Time!

Sugar invented her own board game. She loves playing it with her friends. If you invented something, what would it be? Design your creations here!

Invention #1 Name: _____

Design:

Invention #2 Name: _____

Design:

Invention #3 Name: _____

Design:

MY OWN Club

Austin leads a Bark at the Mail Carrier Club every month. What club would you like to start?

Club Name:

Mission:

Club Members:

fun
with
Kidsm

Draw your club's logo here!

31

My Favorite Veggie

Avril has a vegetable garden full of the most delicious veggies around! If you had your own vegetable garden, what would you grow? What are your favorite and least favorite vegetables?

Favorite Vegetables:

1.
2.
3.
4.
5.

Least Favorite Vegetables:

 1

 2

 3

 4

 5

i ♥ veggies!

Fantastical Forest

There's magic around every corner of the Fantastical Forest. If you look inside the hidden nooks, you'll find some incredible creatures!

Draw this magical location and some of the Beanie Boos who live there.

These Beanie Boos live in the Fantastical Forest:

Kacey   Pixy   Slick

MY ROCK Band

Boom Boom loves rocking out on the drums with her band, Bear Tracks. If you had your own band, what would you name it?

Band Name: _____

Type of Music: _____

Band Members: _____

_____

_____

Write a song for your new band! Don't forget to name it.

Song Name: _Dr. Dow..._

_____

Lyrics: _____

_____

_____

_____

_____

_____

_____

BFF Quiz

Fill out the quiz below for your BFF. If you don't know some of the answers, ask your pal!

BFF

Favorite Animal: _____

Favorite Food: _____

Favorite Song: _____

Favorite Color: _____

Favorite Book: _____

Favorite Actress: _____

Favorite Actor: _____

Favorite Ice-Cream Flavor: _____

Favorite Store: _____

Favorite Musician: _____

Favorite Beanie Boo: _____

Now ask your BFF to fill in your answers!

You

Favorite Animal: _____
Favorite Food: _____
Favorite Song: _____
Favorite Color: _____
Favorite Book: _____
Favorite Actress: _____
Favorite Actor: _____
Favorite Ice-Cream Flavor: _____
Favorite Store: _____
Favorite Musician: _____
Favorite Beanie Boo: _____

World Explorer

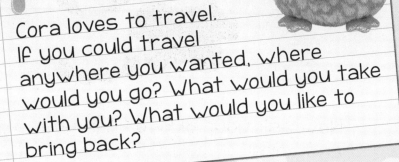

Cora loves to travel.
If you could travel
anywhere you wanted, where
would you go? What would you take
with you? What would you like to
bring back?

Top Five Places I'd Like to Travel:

1

2

3

4

5

Top Five Things I Would Take on a Trip:

1.
2.
3.
4.
5.

Top Five Things I Would Like to Bring Back:

1.
2.
3.
4.
5.

A Few of My Favorite Things

Be Happy!

Some of Daisy's favorite things are playing in the grass, watching the sunrise, and snacking on daisies. What are your favorite things?

1. Art
2. moves
3. foed
4. sholing
5. candy
6. treats
7. Partys
8. Panting
9. reding
10. kides

Costume Time!

Crawly always picks out the perfect Halloween costume. Dream up some Halloween costume ideas here. They can be funny, spooky, or even scary!

Costume Idea #1:

44

Costume Idea #2:

Costume Idea #3:

45

Jokes, Giggles, and Gags

Gilda is one funny flamingo. She's got tons of jokes to tell! She loves making her friends laugh. Write down some of your favorite jokes here!

Favorite Joke #1:

Punch Line:

Favorite Joke #2:

Punch Line:

Favorite Joke #3:

Punch Line:

Your secret Talent

Sammy's hidden talent is that he's a ventriloquist! Yumi's hidden talent is that she can write haiku. What are your hidden talents?

1

2

3

4

5

Three Wishes

Wishful's unicorn horn has magical powers. She can grant wishes with it! What would you wish for?

WISH
#1:

WISH #2:

WISH #3:

Awesome Arctic

The Awesome Arctic is filled with all things winter! Arctic Beanie Boos love playing in the ice and snow.

Draw this cool location and some of the Beanie Boos who live there!

These Beanie Boos live in the Awesome Arctic:

Buckwheat   Ice Cube   Tusk

Awkward Moments

Fluffy blushes all the time. That's why her fur looks pink! Was there a time when you blushed or felt embarrassed? Tell your story here!

My Favorite Fruits

Beaks loves fruit. What's your favorite fruit? What's your least favorite fruit?

Favorite Fruits:

 1

 2

 3

 4

 5

Least Favorite Fruits:

1.

2.

3.

4.

5.

My Favorite Reads

Anabelle loves reading fairy tales. What are your favorite books? List them here!

1 _____

2 _____

3 _____

4 _____

5 _____

6 _____

7 _____

8 _____

9 _____

10 _____

Beanie Boo Fill-in-the-Blank!

Some of the words from the Beanie Boos' personal poems are missing! Can you fill in the missing words?

BOOM BOOM

I'm the coolest,

_____ bear around.

I bang on the drum

and make a big _____!

My favorite time to have lots of

_____

Is when I can run and

_____ in the sun!

MANDY

60

BUZBY

I'm a very _____ bee.

I fly so high it makes me

_____!

On my tippy toes,

I run real _____.

If I'm in a _____

I'll never come last!

SQUEAKER

FLORA

I am _____

and white and pink,

And every now and then

I _____.

I like the night

more than the _____,

So we'll have fun

in _____ways!

ROCCO

spooky Stories!

Haunt is a huge fan of Halloween. Are you? Tell your favorite spooky story here!

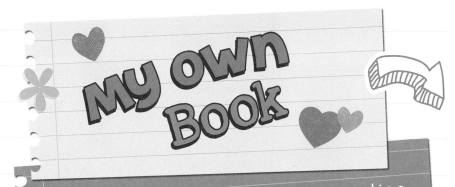

My Own Book

London has an amazing imagination. She imagines she's a writer looking for inspiration for her next novel. If you wrote a book, what would it be called? What would the story be?

My Book Title:

Story:

Draw the cover of your book here:

Movin' on Up

Darci has moved around a lot. She's lived in the Jazzy Jungle, the Mystic Mountains, and the Friendly Field. If you were to move, what are the ten items you would bring with you?

1

2

3

4

5

6

7

8

9

10

Jazzy Jungle

There's always something happening in the Jazzy Jungle, whether it's vine swinging, tree climbing, or just hanging out in the river.

Draw this adventurous location and some of the Beanie Boos who live there.

These Beanie Boos live in the Jazzy Jungle:

Ellie   Kipper   Leona

love it ♥

Favorite Foods

Bamboo is always hungry. That's why he loves food so much! List your favorite foods here:

1 _____

2 _____

3 _____

4 _____

5 _____

6 _____

7 _____

8 _____

9 _____

10 _____

Winter Fun

happy DAY

Glider loves the Winter Beanie Boolympics so much she invented her own event, the Whirl and Twirl Ice Luge. What other events should be part of the Boolympics?

Go for it!

Event Name:

Description:

72

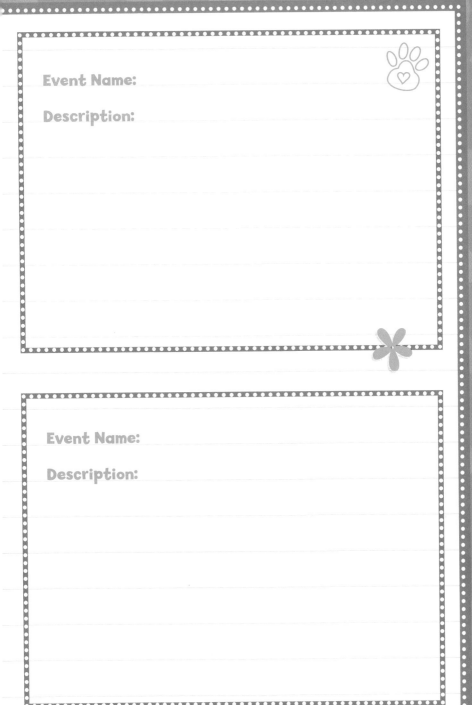

Event Name:

Description:

Event Name:

Description:

You LOVE the Beanie Boos. But which ones are your favorites? List them here!

1
2
3
4
5
6
7
8
9
10

YOUR SUPERHERO Story

Jinxy has a superhero personality called Bat Cat who helps her friends when they're in trouble. Since she's a black cat, sometimes a bit of bad luck follows her. But no matter what, she tries her best to save the day!

BFF

Write a story about the adventures
of Bat Cat!

YOUR Dream Journal

Dreamer's favorite thing is her dream journal. What do you dream about? Write your latest dreams down here!

Dream #1

Dream #2

Dream #3

A New Friend

Honey Bun loves meeting new people and making new friends. When was a time when you made a new friend? Tell the story in the space below.

My Garden

Bloom lives in a flower garden. Draw some of your favorite flowers here. Or make up new ones!

Outrageous Ocean

The Outrageous Ocean might seem big, but there's always a friendly face nearby! In the Outrageous Ocean, the coral reefs are excellent for Hide-and-Boo-Seek.

Draw this wavy location and some of your favorite Beanie Boos who live there!

These Beanie Boos live in the Outrageous Ocean:

Rosie

Aqua

Sparkles

A Delicious Recipe

Muffin loves trying out new muffin recipes. What do you like to bake? Write your favorite recipe and list the ingredients you'll need to make it.

 love it ♡↓

Recipe Name:

Ingredients:

Directions:

87

Holiday Messages

Santa's messenger owls deliver important letters to the reindeer and elves. One messenger, Icicles, delivers these letters all over the Awesome Arctic. What message is Icicles carrying for Santa?

AIR MAIL

Dear Santa,

Top Ten Coolest Jobs

Tusk dreams of becoming a dentist when he grows up. What do you want to be when you grow up? List the top ten coolest jobs here:

1
2
3
4
5
6
7
8
9
10

My Dream Restaurant

Skylar is an amazing chef! He enjoys creating new recipes. If you opened your own restaurant, what would it be called? What would be on the menu?

Restaurant Name:

Type of Food:

Specials:

♥ MENU ♥

Starters

....

....

....

....

Sandwiches

....

....

....

....

Salads

....

....

....

....

Drinks

....

....

....

....

My Favorite Tunes

Aria is a singer whose favorite song is "Owl Always Love You." What are your favorite songs?

1 _____

2 _____

3 _____

4 _____

5 _____

6 _____

7 _____

8 _____

9 _____

10 _____

Time to Hit the Books!

Inky is one of the smartest Beanie Boos around! Her favorite school subject is math. What are some of your favorite subjects?

Favorite Subject #1:

Favorite Subject #2:

Favorite Subject #3:

Subject I'd like to learn more about:

Subject I just started learning:

Silliest Subject:

Most-Fun Subject:

My Fashion Sketchbook

CASHMERE

Love it!

Cashmere dreams of becoming a fashion designer one day! Do you like to create your own styles? Draw some of your designs here!

Friendly Field

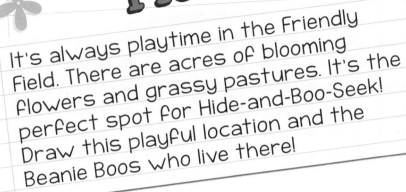

It's always playtime in the Friendly Field. There are acres of blooming flowers and grassy pastures. It's the perfect spot for Hide-and-Boo-Seek! Draw this playful location and the Beanie Boos who live there!

These Beanie Boos live in
the Friendly Field:

Buzby   Sammy   Scooter

protecting the Earth

Sandy and her friends want to help protect their sea home! It's such a beautiful place. How can you protect the environment?

My Magic Spells

Some Beanie Boos believe Serena knows magical spells. If you knew magic, what spells would you like to perform?

Magic Spell #1:

Spell Ingredients:

Magic Spell #2:

Spell Ingredients:

Magic Spell #3:

Spell Ingredients:

Reasons to Be Thankful

Thankful loves eating pumpkin pie. It's one of the things he's most thankful for. What are some things you are thankful for? List them here!

I'm thankful for . . .

1

2

3

4

5

6

7

8

9

10

Facing your Fears

Frights is afraid of his shadow. When he sees it, he gets scared. Write about a time you felt scared. How did you overcome your fear?

ROCK OUT
with Roxie!

Roxie is the DJ of Bear Tracks, the Beanie Boos' band. She likes to spend her free time rocking out with friends. What is her next adventure? Tell her story here!

My Fortune

Jewel uses her gemstone crystal ball to tell fortunes. If Jewel told your fortune, what would it say?

In one year . . .

In five years . . .

In twenty-five years . . .

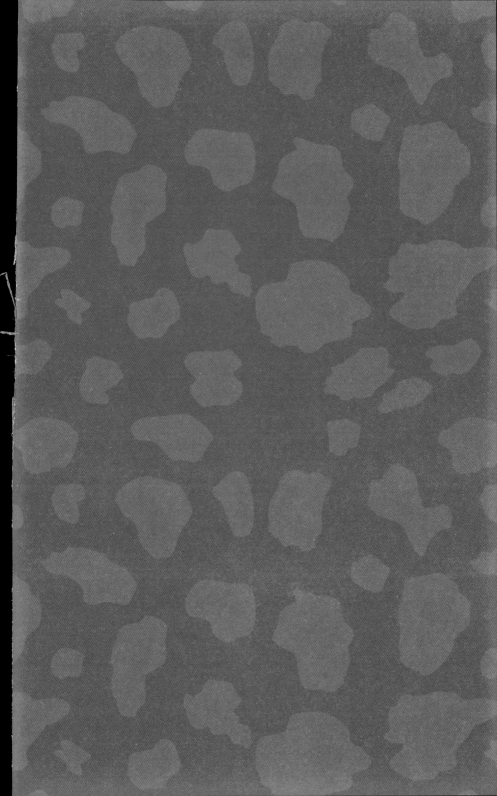

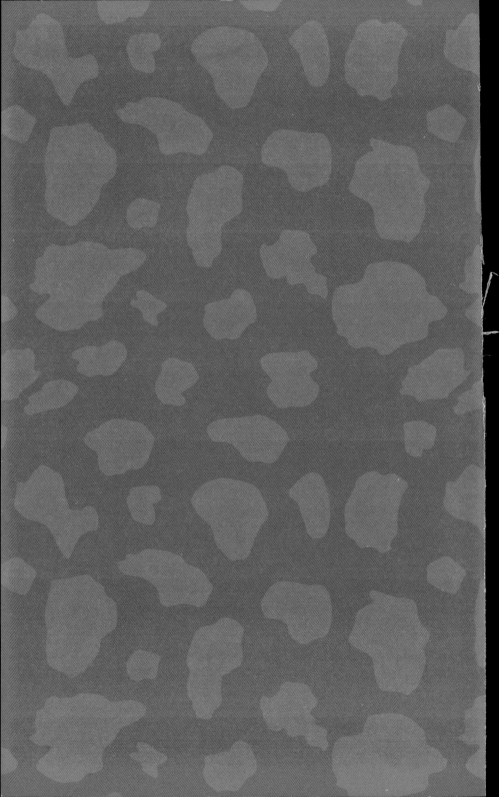